Curious George®

VISITS THE ZOO

Adapted from the Curious George film series
edited by Margret Rey and Alan J. Shalleck

Houghton Mifflin Company Boston

Library of Congress Cataloging in Publication Data
Main entry under title:

Curious George visits the zoo.

"Adapted from the Curious George film series."
Summary: Curious George visits the zoo and manages
to both cause trouble and make up for it in his
inimitable fashion.
1. Children's stories, American. [1. Monkeys—
Fiction. 2. Zoos—Fiction] I. Rey, Margret.
II. Shalleck, Alan J. III. Curious George visits the
zoo (Motion picture)
PZ7.C9219   1985   [E]   85-2415
ISBN 0-395-39036-2

Printed in Hong Kong

DNP   20 19 18

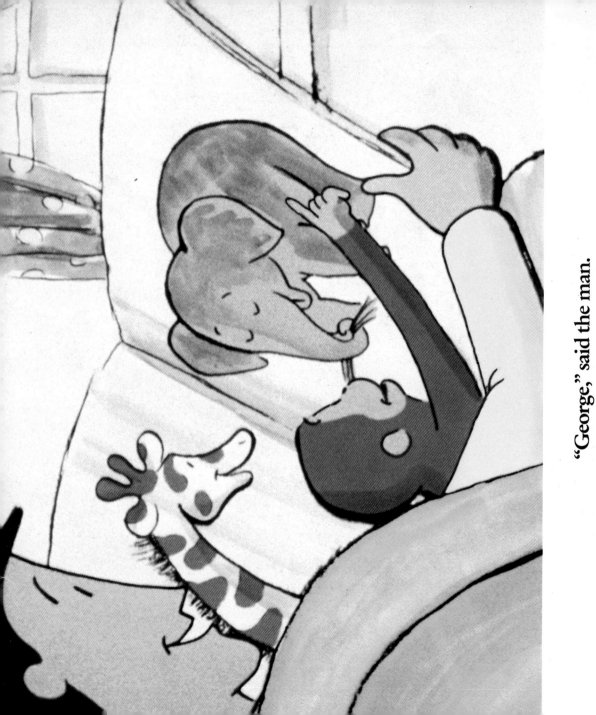

"George," said the man.

"How would you like to see a real elephant? Let's go to the zoo."

There was a lot to see at the zoo.

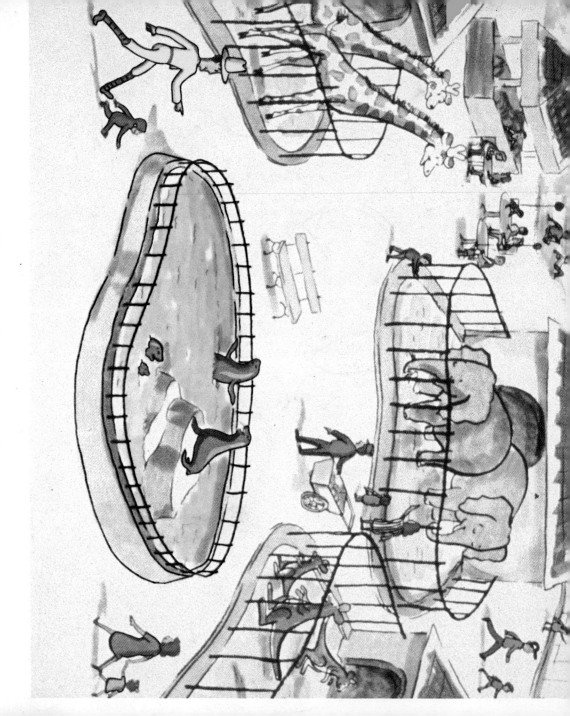

There were the giraffes, with their necks so long they seemed to reach the sky.

There were the kangaroos carrying their babies in a special pocket.

And finally there were the elephants with their floppy ears and their long trunks munching on hay.
It was lunchtime.

People were eating on the park benches

and picnicking on the grass.

"I am going to find out what time they feed the lions," said the man with the yellow hat. "Wait here and don't get into trouble."

While George was waiting, he saw a zookeeper with a pail of bananas for the monkeys.

The keeper put the pail down to get a drink at the water fountain.

George was hungry. He grabbed the pail and ran away with it.

"Hey!" shouted the keeper. "Stop that monkey!"
But George kept on running.

A crowd of people was standing near the monkey house—
just the place for George to hide!

Standing by the cage was a little boy holding a red balloon with a long string.

Suddenly one of the monkeys reached out, snatched the string from the boy's hand,

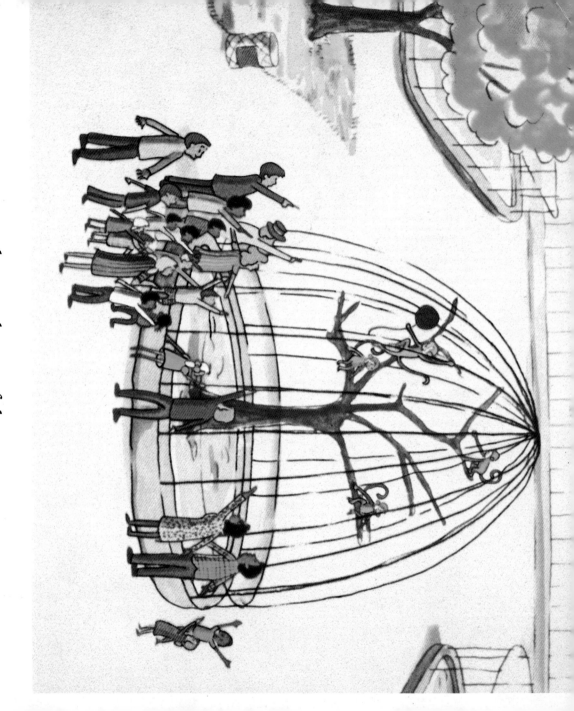

and ran to the top of the cage.

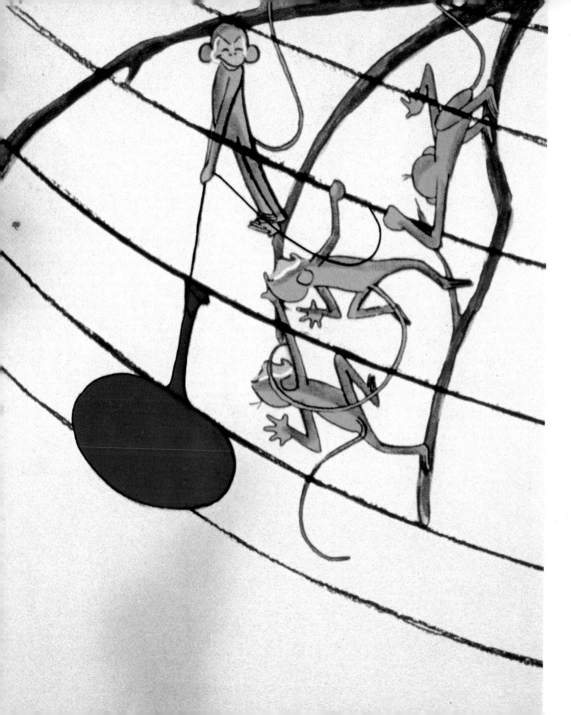

Then he tried to squeeze the balloon through the bars.
The other monkeys started to shriek and scream.

The little boy was crying.

"Please, couldn't somebody get his balloon back?"
asked the mother. None of the people could reach that high.

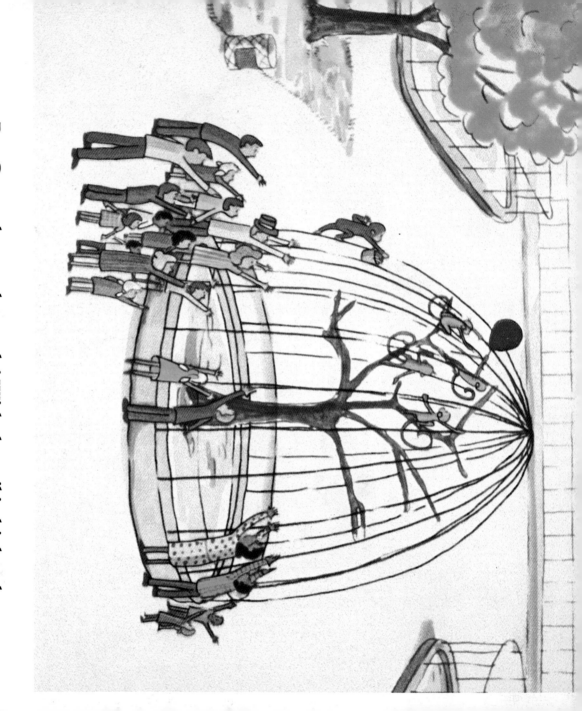

But George knew what to do! With the pail in his hand, he climbed up to the top of the cage.

He took a few bananas and fed them to the monkeys.

While the monkeys were eating, George snatched the balloon and swung down from the cage.

He handed the balloon back to the boy.

Everybody clapped and cheered.

Just then the man with the yellow hat came running. "George!" the man cried, "I have been looking all over for you!"

"Please don't be angry with him," said the mother.
"He saved my son's balloon."

"George should not have taken my pail," said the keeper,

"but he did feed the monkeys."

"And now it's time to feed ourselves, George," said the man.

And that's what they did.